MANUELA ANCUTICI
RUTH PRENTING

I SPY ABC
Totally Crazy Letters!

FIREFLY BOOKS

AND THIS IS HOW IT WORKS

Welcome

There is something here for everyone to discover!

For sleeping bags and eagle eyes,
follow the clues to solve the puzzles.
Did you discover the kite on wheels?
In which letter hides a robot and a cat?
And where can I find the dancing pig?
These are funny colorful Hidden Object Letters -
there is plenty to find and search for.
Be creative, find new ideas
or even more words.

Have Fun!

You will find the solution pages at the end of the book.

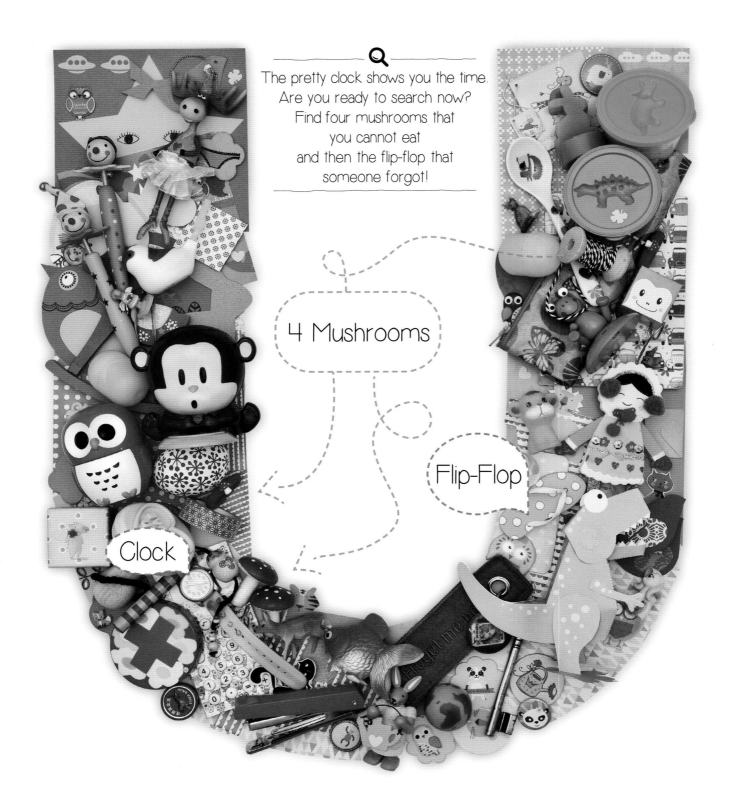

The pretty clock shows you the time.
Are you ready to search now?
Find four mushrooms that
you cannot eat
and then the flip-flop that
someone forgot!

4 Mushrooms

Flip-Flop

Clock

Can you see what I see?
Ten cats, a fox,
seven letters from the alphabet
and a top that keeps spinning.

Mickey Mouse hides here three times
next look for eight vehicles. There is
a hero with his arms stretched up.
Where is the pirate hiding?

If you look carefully
you will find the astronaut.
Do you see Cinderella's shoe?
Find the nine fish fast.

Can you see what I see?
A banana, ice cream in a cone,
two pretzels from the baker
and a croissant, very tasty.

Find three slices of bread,
a pear, four cupcakes and three oranges.
Then look for the two strawberry suckers
on a stick and two waffles to take home.

Can you find the watermelon and five lemons?
Three slices of cheese with holes and
the two limes? Six carrots are hiding here
too along with three clusters of grapes.

Can you see what I see?
A long snake, a starfish, a beetle,
and a yellow lizard that is
very hard to find.

Have you discovered the turtle
that is slowly moving through this letter?
Can you find at least eleven pinecones and
fourteen seashells from the beach?

How nice that I found them first!
Where is the walnut? Can you find the
five feathers as soft as a pillow and
five brown acorns from the forest.

Can you see what I see?
I see two green clover leaves,
maybe they will bring you luck!
There are five small ants somewhere.

The three snail shells are so small
that the three ladybugs could
fit nicely inside. But there would be
no room for the eleven butterflies!

Can you find the three caterpillars?
And look for the two sunflowers,
seven blue flowers and the two
daisies whenever you're ready.

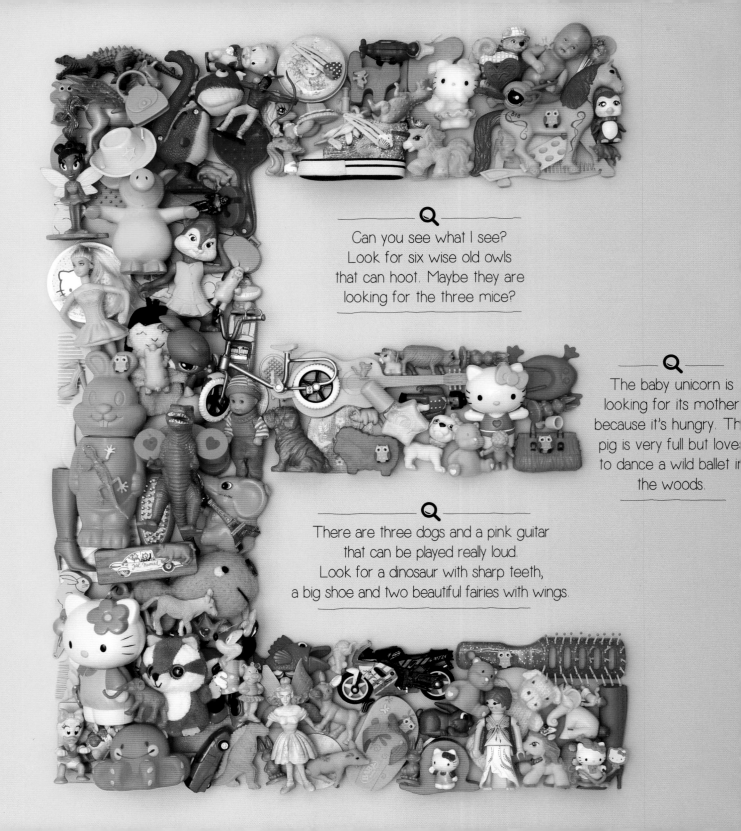

Can you see what I see?
Look for six wise old owls
that can hoot. Maybe they are
looking for the three mice?

The baby unicorn is
looking for its mother
because it's hungry. Th
pig is very full but love
to dance a wild ballet in
the woods.

There are three dogs and a pink guitar
that can be played really loud.
Look for a dinosaur with sharp teeth,
a big shoe and two beautiful fairies with wings.

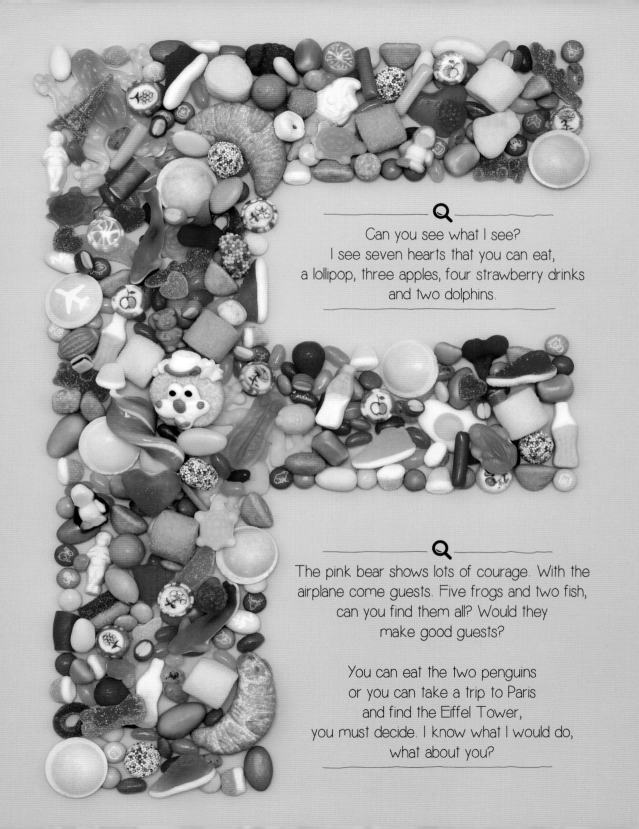

Can you see what I see?
I see seven hearts that you can eat,
a lollipop, three apples, four strawberry drinks
and two dolphins.

The pink bear shows lots of courage. With the
airplane come guests. Five frogs and two fish,
can you find them all? Would they
make good guests?

You can eat the two penguins
or you can take a trip to Paris
and find the Eiffel Tower,
you must decide. I know what I would do,
what about you?

Can you see what I see?
Are you ready to search for the
beautiful letters now? Then find
the hearty H, a flowery W and a giant A.

There are four forks hidden in one letter.
There is a K that looks like the sea
and five stars. Can you find them all?
Please try!

There are two geese in the G
and a gecko. Can you
find the twelve yellow giraffes,
that are hidden in one letter?

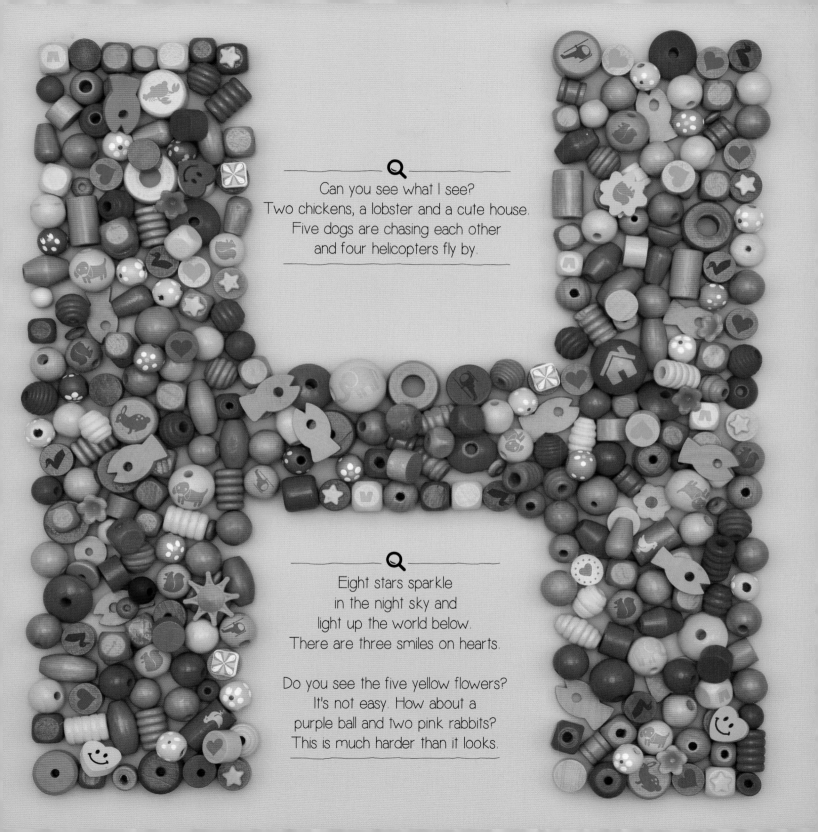

Can you see what I see?
Two chickens, a lobster and a cute house.
Five dogs are chasing each other
and four helicopters fly by.

Eight stars sparkle
in the night sky and
light up the world below.
There are three smiles on hearts.

Do you see the five yellow flowers?
It's not easy. How about a
purple ball and two pink rabbits?
This is much harder than it looks.

Can you see what I see?
Find two dragons, three little pigs,
three elephants, four dwarfs,
and five yellow bears. Was that easy?

Look for a green snail with a whistle.
Who rides the skateboard to the house?
There are five divers and now you've found four
goggles. Maybe now you can take a swim?

There is a lion that bathes in a cup.
Can you find a blue airplane?
If you find a green one too, you win! Now
let's move onto the next letter.

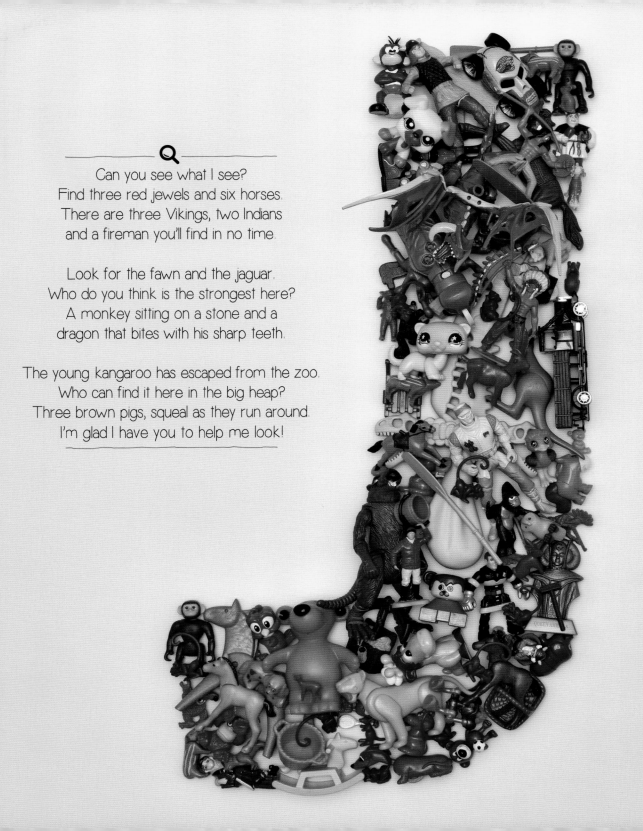

Can you see what I see?
Find three red jewels and six horses.
There are three Vikings, two Indians
and a fireman you'll find in no time.

Look for the fawn and the jaguar.
Who do you think is the strongest here?
A monkey sitting on a stone and a
dragon that bites with his sharp teeth.

The young kangaroo has escaped from the zoo.
Who can find it here in the big heap?
Three brown pigs, squeal as they run around.
I'm glad I have you to help me look!

Can you see what I see?
I see two camels, are they not a
beautiful couple? The yellow parrot
is easy to find, just like the brown rabbit.

The dinosaur wants to eat the dog.
The two motorcycles can travel far.
One tiger sleeps deeply, one is awake.
Eight cars make a lot of noise.

Quickly find the rabbit smiling
and then find the busy little bee.
There is a top, always spinning,
and an astronaut for you to find.

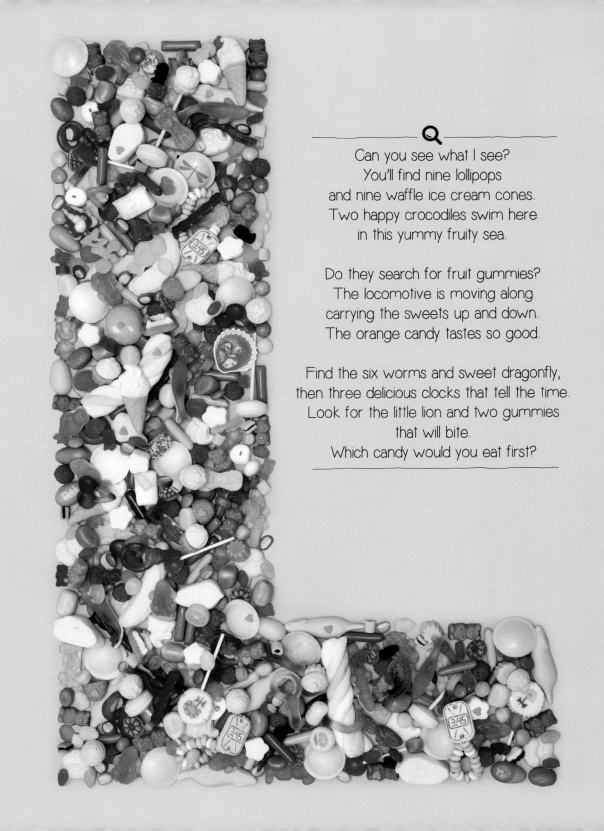

Can you see what I see?
You'll find nine lollipops
and nine waffle ice cream cones.
Two happy crocodiles swim here
in this yummy fruity sea.

Do they search for fruit gummies?
The locomotive is moving along
carrying the sweets up and down.
The orange candy tastes so good.

Find the six worms and sweet dragonfly,
then three delicious clocks that tell the time.
Look for the little lion and two gummies
that will bite.
Which candy would you eat first?

Can you see what I see?
Look, two dolphins from the sea,
plus there is also a beautiful shell.
Look for the two snakes, they've been hiding.

The princess makes a wish.
There is a police car looking for bandits
and fifteen frogs that croak all day.
Can you find the three brushes
for your hair?

There is a beautiful fairy hidden here.
At midnight, the mummy wakes up.
The monkey plays music for us,
while his friend the blue mouse hides.

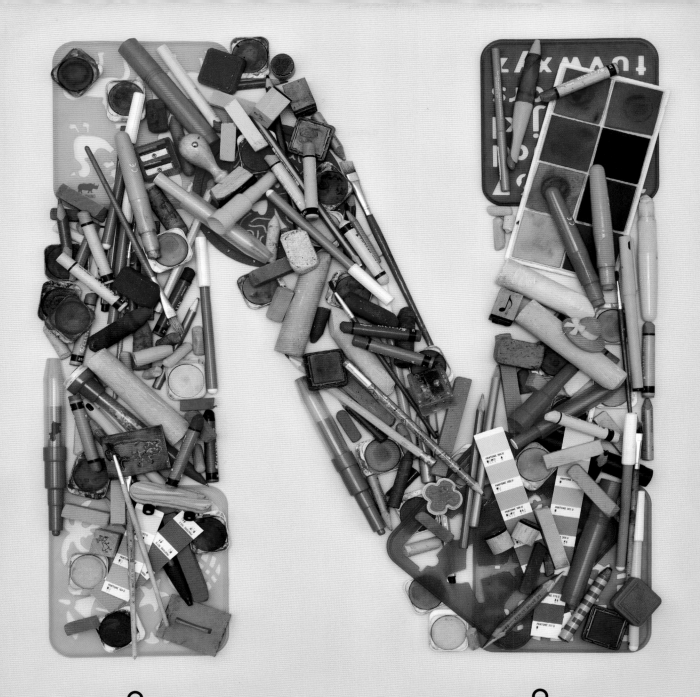

Q

Can you see what I see?
There is a stamp with a pig.
Did you spot the name tag?
Seven brushes are hidden here.

Q

If it gets too bright outside,
get the hat from your house.
Find the little stamp that sings,
the skateboard and the airplane.

Can you see what I see?
Look, a fruit salad, a colorful one.
Do you see the nine hazelnuts?
Five raspberries have been hiding.

Have you discovered the two blackberries?
There are five bright red apples,
which taste good right off the tree
and eight blueberries.

Three figs and a curved banana,
taste good with a cup of cream.
Can you find the fruit that looks like a star?
Find all five, you'll like it very much.

Can you see what I see?
So many vegetables in this bunch.
You can always buy it all fresh.
Can you find four kidney beans here?

Do you like the mini cucumber? Bite it for
good luck. There are three bunches of
broccoli and a yellow pumpkin.
Which one was the easiest to find?

Can you see a large, wild mushroom?
It tastes good on pizza.
Find eight peas that would
be yummy in soup.

Can you see what I see?
Find a snowman and a jellyfish.
Look, you see them here?
Find the hat with the bell.

Two little birds peep quietly.
Are the six owls making a trip?
The fox can see better with glasses.
Can you find the four wheels?

Can you see who is kissing here?
Did you see the friendly lion?
Find a pair of cherries
and ten paper clips.

Can you see what I see?
There is both good and evil.
Three planes, ready to go and a
robot challenge you to find them.

Find thirteen knights who rule the people,
they are wearing protective armor.
The silver shoe might belong to someone.
Can you find two silver forks?

Hidden here are two mice and also
two squirrels for you to discover.
A whale is stranded, thick and big.
What are the two rhinoceroses doing?

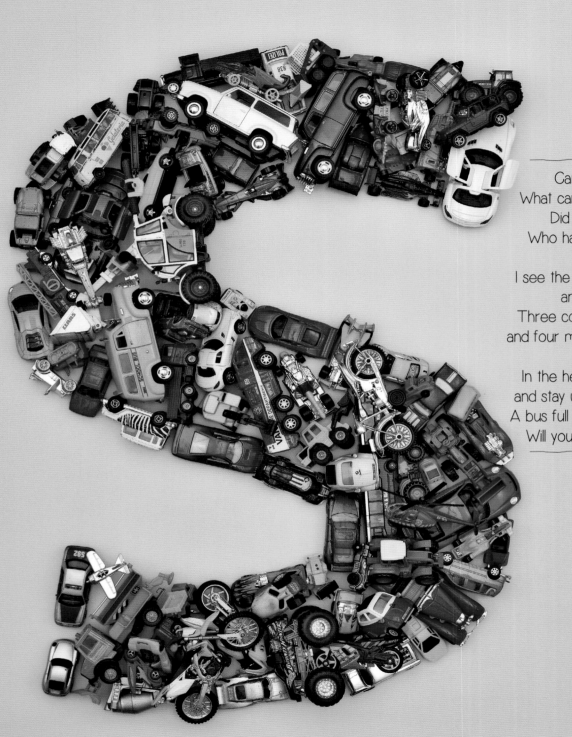

Can you see what I see?
What car will take you home today?
Did you find nine tractors?
Who has found the dragon here?

I see the Jeep that looks like a zebra
and the two firetrucks!
Three convertibles for summer time
and four motorcycles are ready for you

In the helicopter you can fly around
and stay up there, as long as you like
A bus full of ice cream sure looks fine
Will you be the first to buy some?

Can you see what I see?
Thousands of animals from everywhere.
Can you find the eight pigs, five cats
and little tapir look carefully.

The cheetah is the fastest animal.
Can you find four of any of the animals?
There are six crocodiles, three long serpents
and four frogs, who sing in the night.

Two monkeys are dancing in the moonlight.
The giraffe is not fond of being alone.
The hippo and the six tigers
complete the animals you need to find!

Can you see what I see?
The pretty clock shows you the time.
Find four mushrooms that you can not eat.
And who has forgotten their flip-flop?

Look for an old key from the cellar.
A monkey sits on a silver plate.
A moose is ready to dance and there are
two UFOs from space hiding here.

I see a calculator with many owls
and two cats who are meowing.
Do you see the star with only
three points showing?
Count the cars that are parked here.

Can you see what I see?
Discover the first snowflake here
and the four red and white mushrooms.
Find the hidden violin and the
wool monkey who can't stand alone.

A polar bear, a deer and six elephants
that like to travel long distances
to visit distant relatives.
I can see a bracelet with lots of red beads.

There is lots of buttons and thread.
Find the doctor's suitcase.
Ten colorful owls flee to safety.
Do you see ten stars with five points each?

Can you see what I see?
Find two fierce dogs and the grey donkey.
Follow two rabbits to the wonderland,
where you will find an elephant.

Come here, little girl, give me your hand.
Today the sun shines so we go
to the beach. The turtle is not
the fastest animal here, but his friend,
the blue snail, is even slower.

I see purple cubes, there are seven,
and where are the eight pink-colored one
Did you find the small red cat?
There is a ram with very short legs.

Can you see what I see? Look carefully and you'll see the eight hearts and seven purple robots cleverly hiding.

A turtle moves slowly during the day. The bat comes out at night looking for food. Can you find them both?

Four sharks, the terror of the sea, are swimming here looking for you! Much nicer are the four ducks that you can feed along the shore.

Q

Can you see what I see?
So many matryoshkas (Russian dolls).
Who wears yellow and blue on their head?
Find two robots and Master Yoda.

The little fox and the clever little monkey
are here along with three Ganesha.
The ninja is spying on them and
he might make them disappear.

The ghost avoids the sunlight
because it stings his eyes.
The two owls, however, are very smart
and know how to rest during the day.

Can you see what I see?
I see Snow White, along with the Seven
Dwarfs. Mickey Mouse flies around
and sees some people on a roof.

The fire truck quickly puts out the fire.
Heidi plays merrily on the farm.
Where are Red Riding Hood and Pippi
Longstocking hiding? Donald Duck better
hurry or he's in trouble.

The book is almost finished now.
We'll just find Pluto and see
what surprise is on his tail.
Then you're done!

?

Did you find everything?
Here are some
Hints.
Look inside the white circles on
each of the 26 letters.

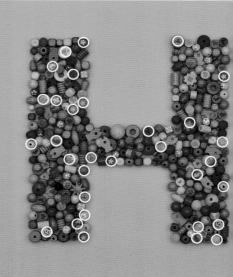

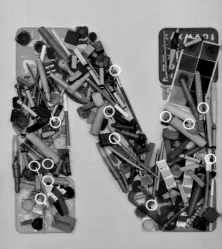

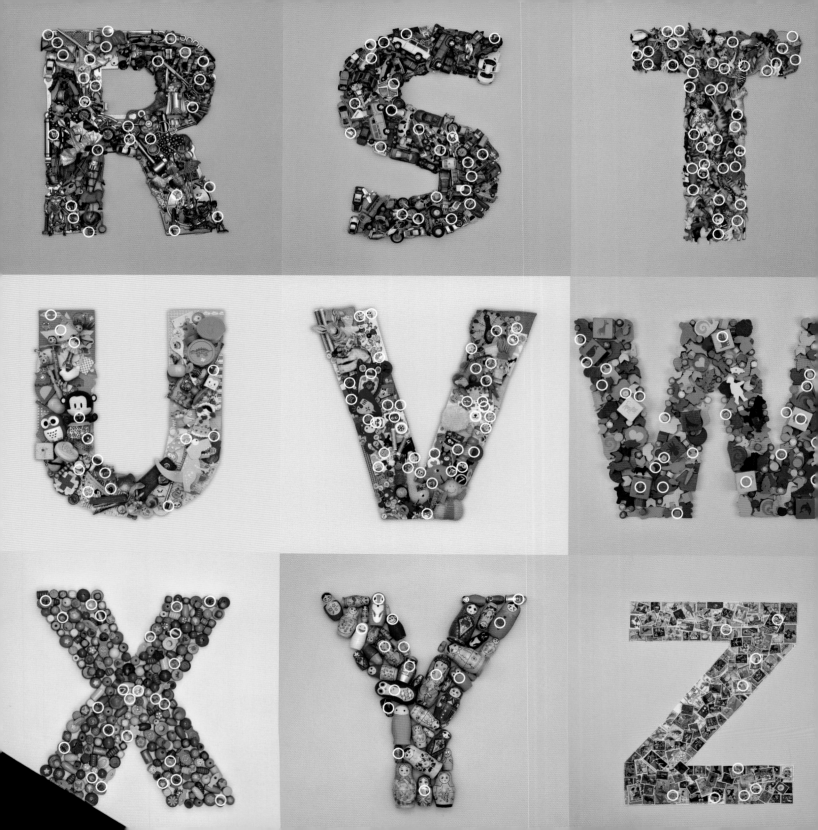

A FIREFLY BOOK

Published by Firefly Books Ltd. 2020

First printing

Library of Congress Control Number: 2020931486

Library and Archives Canada Cataloguing in Publication

Title: I spy ABC / Manuela Ancutici.
Names: Ancutici, Manuela, artist. | Prenting, Ruth, 1972- Ich sehe was, was du nicht
siehst, das verrückte ABC. English.
Description: Previously published as: Prenting, Ruth. Ich sehe was, was du nicht siehst,
das verrückte ABC. English. Buffalo, New York; Richmond Hill, Ontario: Firefly Books,
2017.
Identifiers: Canadiana 20200178628 | ISBN 9780228102625 (softcover)
Subjects: LCSH: Picture puzzles—Juvenile literature. | LCGFT: Picture puzzles.
Classification: LCC GV1507.P47 I2 2020 | DDC j793.73—dc23

Published in the United States by
Firefly Books (U.S.) Inc.
P.O. Box 1338, Ellicott Station
Buffalo, New York 14205

Published in Canada by
Firefly Books Ltd.
50 Staples Avenue, Unit 1
Richmond Hill, Ontario L4B 0A7

Translator: Michael Worek

Printed in China

Editor: Teresa Baethmann
Original German text: Ruth Prenting
Design and composition: Ancutici kommunikationsdesign
Production: Verena Schmynec